Four Sisters

Kimberly Raquel Ward

TATE PUBLISHING
AND **ENTERPRISES**, LLC

Published by Tate Publishing & Enterprises, LLC
127 E. Trade Center Terrace | Mustang, Oklahoma 73064 USA
1.888.361.9473 | www.tatepublishing.com

Tate Publishing is committed to excellence in the publishing industry. The company reflects the philosophy established by the founders, based on Psalm 68:11,
"The Lord gave the word and great was the company of those who published it."

Book design copyright © 2016 by Tate Publishing, LLC. All rights reserved.
Cover design by Niño Carlo Suico
Interior design by Mary Jean Archival

Published in the United States of America

ISBN: 978-1-68237-319-4
1. Family & Relationships / General
2. Fiction / General
16.03.08

To my husband Reggie I love you. Thank you for always encouraging me and pushing me to be better by pursuing my dreams. It means more to me than you can ever imagine.

To our daughter Yolanda, may you find the one God intended for you. Hopefully your father and I can be an example of what a Christ centered marriage looks like in your life.

Sophia

Ek, Ek, Ek! No, the alarm can't be ringing now! Sophia thought. She had drifted off to sleep only two hours before her five a.m. wake-up call. Her three sisters, their kids, and other friends and family had gathered for their annual Moore Family Holiday. Their parents established this holiday when they were kids as a way to instill pride and tradition in their daughters. Each year the holiday was celebrated in the spring when the weather was just right in sunny Florida. She had not thought this out; what had possessed her to agree on hosting the celebration on a night before she was due early at a charity fundraising committee meeting for her foundation for abused and battered women. And why did they insist on having these large gatherings at her house anyway? She lived a comfortable lifestyle but was by no means wealthy. Sophia's thoughts drifted off.

Sophia lived with her husband, Sam, and their twin boys. A veranda wrapped around their four-bedroom home, giving a panoramic view of their acre of land. Sophia's favorite part of the property was an oak tree out front. She and Sam had planted it as a memorial after their eldest son died. She could sit for hours under that tree reading a book and although Sophia did not know it, Sam spent a great deal of time admiring her as she sat out there. She looked so peaceful under that tree, surrounded by God above, and the love she felt from her husband and their three sons. Her thoughts shifted to her family. Oh, her family! Where did she begin? Her oldest sister, Linda, was married with two kids. Next was Victoria, separated and pregnant, no less, and of course Carmen. Carmen, was a newlywed, childless; or at least no children Carmen knew about yet, and naive. Sophia loved her sisters and their diverse personalities despite their crazy marriage escapades.

"OK, wake up now, Sophia!" She shook herself awake, but she just couldn't get up. Finally, after several minutes of replaying last night's festivities, she was able to look over at Sam lying next to her. He was a great man and provider, and he loved Sophia as Christ loved the church. They had been through many ups, downs, and some real loopty loops. But through it all, God had reinforced their marriage. She understood what love is because of the way Sam loved her so deeply. He was her rock, after Jesus, of course.

Sam was also able to sleep through anything, including her alarm. In fact, the night they found out their firstborn was to be heaven sent, Sam had hopped right in bed after a good cry at the hospital. Sophia, on the other hand, had trouble falling asleep between the numbness and misery of never getting to hold their son or see him grow up. She turned her back to Sam, not wanting to wake him, as he wasn't due in the office at the architect/construction firm he ran with his brother until nine. His firm was working on a special project this weekend.

Sophia, on the other hand, had to get cracking if she was to be ready at her post of chief wife and mommy on the home front. After twenty minutes of wavering back and forth, Sophia finally got up to begin her day. Where to begin, she thought. If she had known the plans God had for her that day, she would have stayed in bed!

Linda

Linda had already accomplished working out, feeding her family breakfast, waking up the nanny, and seeing her husband off to work. Currently, she was working on her next business acquisition. All before ten a.m.! Linda was used to this breakneck pace and could not for the life of her understand how her family could relax when there was so much money to be made.

Linda had always been ambitious: graduating valedictorian, completing the top business internships, and having children before thirty. For Linda, being broke meant not having ten thousand dollars in her savings at any given time. As the oldest of Paul and Mary Moore's daughters, she had seen how money and financial struggles had torn her family apart, and she did not want any part of it in her own household. No! She was determined to always be smarter, faster, and more efficient than the next person.

On paper Linda was a great MBA executive with a six-figure salary and city penthouse to boot. But in real life

Linda was missing something. The one area of her life she couldn't figure out or be consistently successful in was her marriage. She had been attracted to Trent, her husband of seven years, ever since she met him in college. His most endearing attribute was his smile. It drove her wild! She was also attracted to Trent because he loved her because of her ambition and no-holds-barred ways. He loved Linda for Linda. And this was her demise. With all her vying to get to the top, her marriage had suffered. Family time consisted of frozen dinners in front of the TV, and intimacy was a luxury for Trent, not her. It had become one of her to dos. Her work consumed her, although it need not too, as Trent did well in his consulting firm, so well Linda could stay home. That's what Trent wanted, but Linda was determined never to depend on a man. No time to dwell on her marriage: she had an eleven o'clock appointment.

Carmen

Carmen had just returned from her honeymoon on the magical islands of Trinidad and Tobago. She and Kelly had a wonderful vacation, and she was in wedded bliss. She thought to herself, so this is what it means to be on a honeymoon, and giggled. She was glad she was in between jobs, having recently graduated a month prior to their wedding, before starting her career as a nurse. They had arrived from the airport the day before in time for the party at Sophia's last night where they received more congratulations, hugs, and kisses all around.

Carmen was looking forward to their first meal together at home, hopefully followed by an intimate evening where she could hone her "skills". She was going to prepare a meal that Kelly would never forget, his favorite foods of mashed potatoes, grilled steak, and asparagus. Little did she know it was a meal she wouldn't want to remember.

She was thinking about how beautiful the evening was going to be, when no sooner than she had placed the steaks on the grill, the doorbell rang. Carmen looked through the peephole and didn't see anything. She thought it was Kelly playing around. She opened the door and found a woman twirling her long brown hair as a baby of no more than six or seven months old tugged on her shoulder. And while the baby was young there was no mistaking that it looked just like Kelly. Carmen's heart dropped. Is this a game, God, or am I being punked, she thought to herself.

As she prayed it was just a coincidence, she asked, "How can I help you?"

"Hi, I'm Susan. Is Kelly around?" The women replied cheerfully.

"Ummm…May I ask what business you have with my husband?"

"Your husband? Kelly, Kelly, Kelly…" the woman said as she shook her head in disbelief. "Your husband is the father to my children—the one I'm holding and another at home with my mother. He's three. Kelly hasn't seen or talked to them in several months, and this is where I tracked him down. I came to see if he is planning on being in our children's lives."

This was just too much for Carmen to handle. The woman's tone that was once cheerful had turned accusatory and how was Carmen to believe a complete stranger over her husband. This was a dream she thought and all she needed to do was wake up!

She closed the door, disbelief surrounding her. What the…What the heck was happening? How was it possible?

She wondered how someone she had given her entire world to never once shared something this intimate. She was his wife for God's sake! Did Kelly seriously think he could live this lie forever? Carmen was starting to feel enraged. Her head was spinning, pounding as her face flushed. Must call sister...It was all she could do to get to the phone. "Hello," she gasped. She could barely get the words out, "Sophia..."

Victoria

Victoria would have never thought in a million years she would be sitting at the clinic alone for her thirty-second-week prenatal appointment, but just a few weeks ago her husband, Grant, had told her that he needed some time and space to think. It seemed like only yesterday they were planning for the baby's future—their daughter's future—where she should go to school, should she take ballet? But no, she sat there alone, waiting for them to call her name for her appointment because her husband had left. She loved her husband, with his stocky build and glasses, a Poindexter type of guy. What she had fallen in love with most was his kind heart that now seemed so distant.

"Victoria." She was still filling out paperwork. "Victoria." She was wrapped up in the thoughts of the happy family life she once had. "Victoria!"

Finally Victoria snapped back to reality. Slowly she got up. "I'm here," she replied in a soft whisper. Victoria had thought she was strong and could do this on her own. She now wished she had brought someone with her. Linda was out because she was always busy. Carmen was still honeymooning. Sophia would have come, but Victoria hadn't asked when she told her about the appointment. Victoria thought all she needed was God, which was true, but He had placed people in her life that she could depend on like her sisters. She knew this appointment might have ominous news as her last ultrasound had to be done again to confirm the findings. Victoria had arrived at the hospital an hour earlier for a level two ultrasound which provided a more detailed view of her womb and the baby growing inside.

The doctor gave her some alarming news: the baby's cord was loosely wrapped around her neck, and they might have to do a C-section before her thirty-eighth week if it tightened or the baby seemed distressed in any way such as a drop in her heartbeat. It was too much for her to handle without Grant around. So many of the decisions she was making on her own she now wished to make with her husband, but her job was to protect their baby, and that is exactly what she was going to do. She decided it was no use trying to figure everything out on an empty stomach, so she went to grab some lunch.

Sophia

"Carmen… Is that you? What's going on? Are you OK?"
"Where to begin?" Carmen inadvertently said out loud. "Sophia, Kelly cheated on me, and he has a three-year-old and a seven-month-old son." Now she could breathe.

Sophia took long a pause as she knew the first words she said were critical. But she really didn't know what to say. "Carmen are you sure; have you spoken to Kelly?"

"Hell no," Carmen blurted out. "Can I come over?"

"Sure," Sophia said, "That's what the extra room is for. Before you come, I need to ask you an important question. She again asked, "Have you and Kelly talked?"

"He's the last person I want to see. No, we have not talked. He went to run a few errands."

"OK, you can come over and clear your head, but then Kelly and you need to talk," Sophia stated firmly.

Carmen's head was spinning: honeymoon, babies, lies, deceit. This was too much for one person to handle. She quickly hung up, packed a bag, and dashed over to her sister's house. How could this be? They had met in school over a year ago and were so in love or so she thought. At this point she didn't care if Kelly came home and found her missing. It was the least he deserved. Scum, she thought, just scum.

Victoria

Separated, eight months pregnant and facing a C-section which was not a part of the birth plan she had imagined. Victoria was sitting at her favorite café contemplating what she should do. Call Grant.

The phone rang a couple of times. "Hello?" the voice stumbled on the phone. He must be with someone she thought. She knew how he answered the phone when they were together.

"Grant its Victoria. We need to talk."

"What do you want, Victoria?" Grant asked.

"It's about the baby."

"What about the baby?"

"Grant, please come and meet me at the café where we first met. We need to talk."

"Fine. Give me an hour."

Victoria sighed. How had they gotten so off track? They were pillars in the community, always doing the Lord's work, helping, and encouraging, inspiring, giving money to whoever they saw in need. Maybe that was the problem. They were so wrapped up in others' lives that their own became neglected. When it happened she didn't know. They had been married four years, and in that time date nights, sex, romance, and just being together had dwindled. But their social calendar was full—always a party, cause, or fundraiser to attend. Well, enough about that, Victoria decided. She wanted to eat her lunch in peace before Grant came roaring along.

Sophia

"OK, Lord, my sisters are really going through it right now. Carmen with Kelly, Linda with Trent, Victoria with Grant; all their marriages seem to be going in different directions instead of toward each other. What do you want me to do?" she asked out loud. "Got it. We'll have a girls' getaway, just the four of us, to reconnect, talk, and pray." Prayer was vital to Sophia. There had been days after her miscarriage that she didn't feel like living, doing, or breathing. On those days talking to God is the only way she had survived.

She continued tidying up the room Carmen would stay in when she felt the brush of something familiar yet exciting. It was her hubby. He came up behind her and ran his hand along her back in a gentle caress. Man, she thought, he drives me crazy. Sophia responded by turning around and planting a nice sensual kiss on her husband's lips. He whispered in her ear, "Don't start nothing you can't finish." She smiled and lead Sam to their bedroom. It would be at least thirty minutes before Carmen arrived, plenty of time if they got this party started. He began to kiss her deeply and passionately so that her whole body quaked and shivered. She felt the passion burning down deep within her. Then she blanked and was taken into wedded bliss with her groom. This was the way God intended it to be.

Carmen

Carmen arrived at her sister's house at 7:59pm. She wished she could erase the last two hours or so. Sophia was glowing when she answered the door. Carmen knew that glow. In fact, she had just experienced it on her honeymoon. Now she was miserable, but she was happy for her sister. At least someone was enjoying being married. She hugged Sam, kissed her nephews, and headed upstairs to where her sister had a pot of hot tea and lemon waiting as well as a journal, fresh pillows, and ice cream…cookies and cream— her favorite.

Sophia gave her a few minutes alone and then joined her after kissing her sons goodnight. She didn't say a word. That was not Sophia's way. She allowed you to open up. She just sat beside Carmen and held her. Then the tears started to come. They trickled at first, and then they came pouring out in sobs. The initial shock was over. She called Kelly on her way over to let him know where she would be. She had a change of heart about just disappearing as she still felt a sense of duty to her husband. When he asked why and for how long, at the mention of Susan's name he understood immediately and began to profusely apologize. For Carmen it was too little too late. How could he deny his children and then get married falsely? She told him she would be in touch, but not to contact her, and instead get on his knees and pray. Kelly sounded defeated but agreed.

Sophia

Sophia had never ever seen her little sister so distraught. How could she help her? She knew she couldn't take away the hurt, so she held Carmen and let her sob uncontrollably for an hour. Then, she tucked her in just as she had done when they were kids and gave her some hot tea. Tomorrow she would try to get the girls together and talk about the sister powwow. Tonight she needed solace and comfort in the arms of her husband. Sam was still her sounding board after all these years. Wise counsel indeed! She would pitch her idea to him and see what he suggested.

Sophia tiptoed out of the guest bedroom and down the hall to where her beautiful twin boys slept peacefully. She was still in awe that such beauty could come after such tragedy. The tragedy of what could have been. She became misty-eyed and weak. What is this world coming to? she thought. Husbands leaving their pregnant wives to fend for themselves, married couples taking unnecessary jabs at each other and acting like it's OK or cheating and covering it up for so long! "Why, Lord, why?" she cried out deep within her soul. "I don't understand."

As she walked to their master bedroom, she felt the Holy Spirit telling her to rest in His peace because, after all, He is the Prince of Peace.

Sophia was exhausted, but as usual, Sam was waiting for her with a cup of chamomile tea. "Come here, baby," he said, soft and deep. She complied readily and melted in his arms. "I love you," was all she could manage. He could see in her eyes she was emotionally done. He began to caress and massage her until the two became one. Sophia laid peacefully in the loving arms of the man she loved, her best friend, husband, provider, and father to their three beautiful children. She drifted off, but not before thinking about the mess each of her sisters were facing.

Victoria

Victoria was not so lucky. As Sophia laid in her husband's arms, she was tossing, turning, fighting for sleep after the meeting she had with Grant. How did their relationship deteriorate so far? She did not know. They were like strangers. He heard the medical procedures, the advice, but acted like a robot. She told him how the doctor said if their daughter was still in jeopardy of being born with the cord around her neck they would suggest proceeding with a C-section. Grant knew how Victoria felt about, needles, hospitals, and procedures. She did not like them and they made her feel like she was losing control of her birthing experience. Yet he just sat there like a robot and not even engaging in the conversation. She was reeling inside. Why God? Why me? I mean, I don't get it. I go to church. I pay my tithes. I attend Bible study every week, and my marriage is in shambles? I'm even on the usher board. "Why me?" she shouted. She didn't care who heard. She was desperate.

Then a thought quickly came to her. You are not married to me. You are married to the church, its functions, the appearances, and the entire hubbub surrounding ministry. But when is the last time you sought me out about my will in your life and in your marriage?

Wow! Victoria had to take a long, hard look at herself. OK, Lord, I hear you. I'm too exhausted to argue right now. Just let me get some sleep, and we will talk in the morning. To fall asleep, she began imagining the way her life used to be.

Linda

Linda's day had been pretty routine, until after dinner, and that was the way she liked it. She had crushed the competition at her 11:00 a.m. appointment by completing a successful merger and acquisition with an international company, and still got home to feed the kids their favorite frozen lasagna and talk to Trent.

Trent. She thought about the one relationship that failed her, the one that should not. She contemplated this fact as she lay in the guest bedroom, which made daydreaming about her male coworkers a lot easier. She had been sleeping in this guest bedroom for months. First it was here and there when she worked late from home as to not disturb Trent when she was finished. Then it became routine as the couple drifted apart and Trent asked her to choose their marriage or her work. She choose the intense acquisition she was working on that night and never looked back. Not that she would ever cheat on her husband. The scandal and fallout would be too much to handle. But dreaming—that was harmless—she thought. She looked but didn't touch. That was her policy, especially since some of them were married. What's the harm she had thought?

But seriously, Trent and Linda's separate lifestyle was taking its toll. They were not only sleeping in separate beds, driving separately, and they didn't even hang out with their mutual friends or date each other anymore. The only thing they shared nowadays was bank accounts. She remembered the old days when they were just starting out. When date night was pizza and burgers. When entertainment was each other, and where hard and unkind words were not uttered. Now they had arrived. Everyone envied them and wanted to be like them. Little did they know that behind closed doors Trent and Linda were shells of their former selves. It was so bad that Trent served Linda divorce papers after dinner. And that's when her routine became anything but normal. Without a word or warning he just handed her the papers and said goodnight to her. Now she lay there contemplating where it all had gone wrong while her husband was in the next room.

Sophia

The next day Sophia woke up refreshed and ready to plan the sisters' retreat. What a Friday night. She was raring to go, so she thought long and hard about what type of trip they should have and what they should do. Sam loved her idea and agreed it was a good time for them to get away but cautioned her on the length of time as Victoria was quickly approaching her due date. Before she started planning the details of the trip she called her office and let them know the committee meeting would be rescheduled for the fundraiser as they had more time and it was a few more months away. First and foremost, they needed to get out of town. Everybody needed a little perspective on their respective situations. Secondly, they needed time: time to relax, relate, and reflect on where their lives were heading. Sophia decided a month was a good amount of time, but she wasn't sure if her sisters would agree to how they spent that month. For that, she would have to give them a call. "Mom," she heard one of the twins say. Duty calls, she thought. I'll talk to my sisters this afternoon.

Sisters

Meanwhile, Carmen did not wake up until noon. After tossing and turning most of the night, it was a wonder she had gotten any rest. She needed to get away, she thought, clear her head. How funny she had just come from this romantic getaway that was built on a lie. She hated, yes hated, Kelly so much right now. She did not want to see him for a long time.

Linda was at work again on Saturday. At the moment she was physically home, but her mind was on another merger that she must handle this weekend. It has reached the point where even my career is not satisfying, she thought. I've worked so hard to get here, sacrificing my family, time, marriage, and now I feel so empty. I wish I had enjoyed the journey. Trent came up behind her, interrupting her thoughts. He missed his wife. With everything going on in their lives surrounding work, kids, and family he still thought of Linda as his home; and when he was unsure of himself as he was now after serving her divorce papers, he wanted to hold her and feel the way they use too. She tensed. He felt his wife's apprehension and just walked away. Why bother even trying? He thought. Why bother?

Victoria woke up early and headed to church. It was the only place she could find peace lately and keep her mind off her situation. Today was a volunteer activity for the youth in need. She was so distraught she thought helping others might keep her mind occupied. The church had a community garden that they allowed the youth to manage. She was ready to get planting and sowing seeds both physically and spiritually.

After lunch, Sophia settled into her favorite chair and began to jot down some notes about what she wanted to go over with her sisters. The morning had gotten away from her. At the last minute she realized her five year old twin boys had baseball practice that she needed to take them to.

The trip would be one month, a time for each sister to get away and reflect as well as refresh and renew. In that time they would have planned and unplanned activities as well as group excursions along with alone time. At the resort and spa they would visit for the last week of their retreat they would make decisions about the direction of their lives and marriages.

Sophia decided she would call Victoria first. As a middle child like herself, she was more "go with the flow" than their other two sisters were. If she could convince Victoria, then Victoria could convince Carmen as they were closer in age, and Sophia could talk to Linda. First things first she hadn't talked to Victoria since her ultrasound appointment and she wanted to know how that went. "Hello Victoria," Sophia greeted her.

"Hi, sis," Victoria replied dejectedly.

"How are you? How was the doctor's appointment?"

"It was as great as could be expected." Sarcasm tinged Victoria's answer.

"Oh my, I'm sorry, sis," Sophia said. "Well, I'm calling you because I think we all could use a getaway."

"A getaway? From what? Work, home, husbands, reality- why is that needed?" Victoria stated curtly. "Whatever gave you that idea? I mean I'm perfectly happy doing my church work, ministry, and living separately from my husband, I mean what woman wouldn't be enjoying some alone time before her child was born." Victoria rattled on.

"Exactly." Sophia tried to remain positive, but her sister's negativity was taking its toll. "Meet me for tea at States Square in an hour?" "My treat?"

"Sure," Victoria replied before hanging up the phone. "But I make no promises," she added.

They met an hour later in the cool, crisp afternoon outside of States Square the premier tea house in town and the one which the sisters loved going to when they wanted to spend time together. The art of teas was severely lacking, but States Square got it right Sophia thought as she approached her sister and gave her a big hug. Victoria looked disheveled, not like herself, and frankly, gaunt, despite her pregnant belly. One would think she was a sickly woman.

They sat down and ordered a pot of hot jasmine passion fruit tea for two, cucumber sandwiches, and strawberry and blueberry scones. Victoria had tears in her eyes but could not cry. All her emotion was bottled up in her, unable to come out. Sophia could see the pain in her sister's face and hated to see her like this. It hurt her.

After Victoria filled Sophia in on the emotionally trying last twenty-four hours with the doctor and Grant, they enjoyed their tea and food. Sophia broached the sisters' getaway by stating, "Well, you know, that's why we all need to get away, including myself."

Victoria rolled her eyes as she angrily said, "What do you have to get away from? Your life is perfect!"

Perfect? Sophia thought. Far from perfect her thoughts continued. Losing your firstborn is not perfect. Being jealous of others when they were able to get pregnant while you waited is not perfect. Crying yourself to sleep every night for months after the tragedy of losing her baby! She hated that word. She had not misplaced him; he was taken from her! Avoiding the affections of your husband and having her own insecurities when she became pregnant again and then when she started her foundation. Yes, my life is perfect! What do I have to complain about? Sophia understood where her sister was coming from, Victoria was unable to be happy for another, because she had been there before, and she still found herself there if she became less than content with her own life.

She responded gracefully to her sister. "You know as well as I do that nobody's life is perfect, but there are perfectly beautiful moments, and I just happen to be enjoying a lot of those right now. I'm sure the storms and trials will come, and when they do, I want to be prepared by being renewed. That's why I think this is a good trip for us. My idea is to rent a beach house a couple hours away for three weeks and then the fourth week go to a resort and spa. During that time I pray we all have time to rest, reflect, and meditate on the Word of God regarding each of our situations and where we are heading. I also want us to have lots of fun, laughter and connect as sisters."

Victoria's tears were ready to spill onto her cheeks. "That sounds wonderful. Sign me up! I definitely need to clear my heart and my head. When can we go?"

"Well, that depends on you," Sophia smiled. "Since you are the new mommy, and your due date is quickly approaching, I would suggest you get approval from your doctor. We will only be an hour or two away so in case something happens we can get you back ASAP."

"OK," Victoria said with new vigor. "I'll call my doctor. Since I'm eight months pregnant, we better leave soon, like Saturday," she giggled. All of a sudden she was joyful. That was the Victoria Sophia knew.

"OK, it's settled. You check with your doctor, and in the meantime I'll talk to Linda. Can you talk to Carmen?" she asked.

"Sure," Victoria replied. Although she had her own problems, it was nothing compared to what Carmen was going through: newlywed and a stepmother to boot. That was tough. Sophia had briefly filled Victoria in on all that had transpired between Carmen and Kelley so Victoria could be sensitive to her sisters state of mind when she talked to her about the trip.

They settled their bill, hugged, and each walked off in a different direction with renewed purpose.

Linda

"Back at work on this fine Monday morning?" her secretary said.

"I never left," Linda muttered through clenched teeth. She wondered why she did this to herself. All weekend she had been tied up in that merger. She would share in fifty percent of the profits, but it had a cost of missing her daughter's recital. She didn't even want to think about the look on her family's faces, especially Trent's blank stare as she told them she would not be joining them. Another parenting and marriage fail.

She just needed to get through this week and try to do damage control this weekend. Maybe I'll cook dinner, she thought. I know. I'll make Trent's favorite, chicken cacciatore. Her thoughts were interrupted as her sister came through her office door. "What in the world are you doing here?" She let her astonishment slip out in her tone.

Sophia smiled and sweetly replied, "I'm here to see you."

"But don't you have to work?" Linda questioned.

"I'm working right now." Sophia looked her sister directly in the eyes. "Sit down."

She sure has a way with words, Linda thought. "Listen," she said as she sat behind her desk. "I have a lot to get done and a tough week ahead."

"This will take only a few minutes and is precisely why I'm here," Sophia stated. "You are so busy, too busy, for family, friends, and fun, not to mention your sisters. You look worked up, and from what I've been hearing lately, or lack thereof, things are not so good between Trent and you right now."

How could she know that? Linda thought.

Sophia answered her unasked question. "I know my sister. When things are great, you brag to anybody who will listen, but when they aren't, you get real quiet."

They sat in silence letting the quiet hang in the air.

Linda spoke after Sophia filled her in the need for retreat with her sisters and how it would give everyone some perspective in their lives. "Yes, that sounds like a great idea," Linda relented after having given Sophia a lengthy list of why any of them shouldn't go such as Victoria being so far along in her pregnancy and her hectic work schedule. But then she began to see the beauty of getting away from it all. After all she had plenty of vacation time as she was always working. She was tired, tired of fighting for a marriage that she didn't even know was worth fighting for. "When do we leave?"

"Well, once Victoria gets the go-ahead from her doctor, we can leave this Saturday. We will meet at my house and drive to the beach house. Once there we will have planned and spontaneous activities for us to relax, reflect, and refresh for the first three weeks. The fourth week we will go to a resort and spa nearby so we can just relax and unwind before coming back to our families.

"Wow, you really thought this out," Linda commented.

"Yes. I really want all our lives to be directed for a purpose."

"Agreed," Linda stated as her cell phone registered a text message.

"I'll call you once I hear from Victoria."

"No need," Linda said. "We all just received a group text that everything is a go from her doctor as long as we stay within an hour's reach of him. She will still need to attend her weekly appointments but he will give her a thorough work up this week before the trip with an ultrasound and plan to do Skype appointments unless her medical status becomes more acute. In which case he will provide a colleague she can go to while we are away. Once he knows specifically where we will be."

"Great!" Sophia exclaimed "So we'll use this week to get our affairs together and talk with our families."

My family...Linda drifted off in thought. Imagine the conversation between me and Trent.

"Well, I love you, sister."

"I love you too." Linda walked her sister out.

Carmen

Carmen thought that this week had started out rough, but she was really excited to get away. Since she was in between jobs she didn't have to worry about requesting time off. She only had to talk to Kelly. Kelly, the scumbag of a man who had left his family responsibilities for another woman. She was furious again. She couldn't go on this trip without hearing him out. As usual her big sister Sophia had been right, Kelly and her needed to talk. Well, she wanted to listen, listen to what he had to say for himself. She texted Kelly, "WE NEED TO TALK." In all caps. She quickly received a reply, simply "OK." My, what my marriage has come to.

Carmen met Kelly at a local park. She waited for him on a bench near a wooden bridge that crossed over a brook before it ran into the lake. She couldn't believe how nervous she was to see her own husband. The anticipation was killing her. Her heart quickened as he approached. Tall, dark, hand... No, she thought. Liar, cheater, deadbeat are more accurate descriptions. Nonetheless, she had chosen to marry this man for better or worse, and this was definitely worse. God help me, she thought. "Carmen," Kelly's deep voice interrupted her thoughts.

Sophia

Everybody met at Sophia and Sam's house at nine Saturday morning. The excitement was palpable. None of them had been away from her family longer than a few hours. And defiantly not to focus on their lives and needs. It was new for everyone, especially Sophia. She had awakened extra early that morning and prayed for each of her sisters, their marriages, and their families. It was crazy to believe that a few short years ago Sophia was a mess because she was so distraught over the loss of their son. She wept and wept and wept. She didn't feel like living or going on, but God met her in that place so uniquely that she was thankful for her salvation and that she could rely on Him fully. It was the only thing that truly got her through. She knew that it was all going to work in her favor, just as Romans 8:28 states.

After her morning devotional, she and Sam spent some quiet time together. She was so in love with her husband. Even though they did not always see eye to eye, they loved each other more than life itself. They loved the way each other's mind worked, their take on the world, their caring spirit, and affection for each other. They were truly living the dream.

Carmen

Carmen woke up early at her sister's house to finish packing. After her lengthy talk with Kelly last night in which he apologized more times than she could count, he actually encouraged her to go. She was shocked. Why would he want her to leave when they were in the middle of a crisis? His reasoning was that they needed a break from each other. They had agreed not to contact each other during Carmen's time away unless they absolutely needed to. Kelly would, however, come to Sophia's house with the rest of the family to see Carmen off.

Victoria

Grant was not coming. She slammed the phone down. His eight-month-pregnant wife was on her way out of town for some R and R, and he could not put his differences aside to come see her off! She was upset. So upset she slammed a second time just thinking of their exchange. Victoria called Grant but her call went straight to voicemail, when she tried to call the phone again, she received a text that he was busy and not able to see her off but hoped she had safe travels.

How did it get like this? She wondered again. There was a time when she and Grant were inseparable, and then she got involved in church. A thought entered her head. It wasn't so much she got involved in church, but it was the fact that she got involved in every aspect that had bothered Grant. Date nights became less of a priority when church events and outreach would crop up, and they needed volunteers. Victoria would step in. Then, she became pregnant, and Grant was so excited, like overly excited, and she couldn't figure out why. She later found out, from a church member no less, it was because he thought that would mean she would slow down. The opposite became true. Once the first trimester was over, she went into full-throttle mission-mode work. She was rarely home, and when she was, she was wishing she was at church. Grant became more of a roommate than a partner.

The situation continued downhill until one day after Bible study she came home to find he was gone—like cleared his side of the closet gone—and it looked like he had left in a hurry. As Victoria took the time to think about it, and after some self- reflection she realized her husband had been pleading with her to choose their marriage and relationship over the church long enough, but she hadn't listened. Now, when she needed him most, he wasn't there, and neither was anybody from the church. The irony was not lost on her.

Linda

Trent was happy for Linda to go. Giddy, in fact. She had thought for sure he was going to say no. Instead, he said he would hold off on the divorce papers until after their trip. He would bring the kids to see her off but wait in the car, and, true to his word, on Saturday morning that's exactly what he did.

The car ride was long and tense. What do you talk about with someone who wants to leave your marriage? Linda knew she was not innocent in this. She had left the marriage a long time ago when she chose career over home. The kids were aware something was not right between their parents and were unusually quiet. Once at Sophia's house, they jumped out to meet their cousins. Trent, the good man that he was, helped Linda with her bags and then gave her a hug. His warm embrace touched every fiber of her body and sent her spine tingling. She knew love was still there. She just had to figure out how to get back to it.

After the SUV was loaded up, all the sisters said their goodbyes to their parents and respective families. They headed out on the open road ready for adventure, each of them lost in thought about how this trip would go and if or when they would be changed. The possibilities were brimming with promise.

They arrived at the beach house at eleven o'clock after a restroom stop. As they pulled up, they were immediately captivated by the quaint two-story house with its white shutters and blue trim set against the backdrop of the ocean and sand. It was gorgeous. They unloaded the car, stepped inside, and were greeted by a tray of assorted nuts, fruits, and cheeses as well as cold water, ice tea, and wine. The open kitchen stretched across the length of the house, its granite countertops divided by a large stainless steel fridge, range, and farmhouse sink. They walked the travertine floor into the adjacent living room and took in the flat screen TV, fireplace, two oversized pale blue chairs, love seat, and couch before moving to the large veranda that wrapped around the house where they stood in awe into the deep blue ocean. They explored the two downstairs and two upstairs bedrooms, along with the lounge and small library. After the sisters had settled in, unpacked and took a nap they all came to the kitchen to see what Sophia had arranged for the evening.

Sophia

A decadent spread of fruits, cheeses, dips, hors d'oeuvres, veggies, crackers, snicker doodles, and chocolate cupcakes, along with sparkling white grape juice, covered the counter. Candles flickered, and light jazz music was playing in the background. The sisters were speechless.

"Ladies, I wanted us to have a fun, carefree night," she said, breaking their trance. "We are here to rest, reflect, and hopefully reevaluate our lives and where God is taking us. I want this to be a time where we pause and possibly change directions. I have a journal for each of you to write down things that may be happening in your lives or that you experience and learn from this trip. Take some time each day to meditate and write down what you feel the Holy Spirit is saying." Sophia passed out the journals. Inside each of them she had written a short yet poignant letter to that sister.

The rest of the evening the sisters laughed, cried, ate, and enjoyed each other's company. They all felt closer and more connected to each other than they ever had before. Each sister headed to their room, it had been an eventful day and they needed their sleep but before doing so each sister read her journal. Sophia stayed behind to tidy up before heading to her room as well.

Linda

Dearest Linda,

You are a vibrant young woman with great ambition. That drive has afforded your family many opportunities but lately I have seen that ambition become a detriment to your family. I love you and want nothing but the best for you. I pray this trip helps you find perspective and balance in the only place it can be found: in our Savior and Lord Jesus Christ. May God bless you and guide you.

Love, Sophia

Carmen

Little sister,

My, what major life events you are experiencing now at such a young age and time in your marriage. My prayer for you is that you do not lose that youthful outlook and newness of marriage given the circumstances. I know this is not what you signed up for, but marriage never is exactly what we had imagined. Most of us, me included, get caught up in the glitz and glamor of the wedding day, but that is just a brief moment in the tapestry of the lives God is weaving together. I cannot begin to understand why this is happening, but I can tell you that now more than ever you must fully rely on God. It will be hard, but we all are here for you and praying over you. Little sister, I love you, and remember that the weak will be made strong through Christ Jesus.

Love, Sophia

Victoria

My middle sister,

I love you and the mother you are becoming so much. You are one strong lady, and I admire you. I admire how you continue to have grace under pressure when all else seems to be falling around you. I worry, though, that you've become legalistic in your interactions with God. It is good, and we are called to serve the church body, but not at the detriment of our families. The first institution God established was the family—husband and wife—in Genesis, which shows just how important it is. My prayer for you is that you find and reconnect with God on a more spiritual level and that this journey will reveal to you how to reconnect and reconcile with Grant. I know you two love each other and love that baby growing in your womb.

Love, Sophia

Sophia

Dear Sophia,

God; you and I have been rolling along with each other for a while. May this journey bless you and keep you and show you the next steps in your life. May you and God become so intertwined that you know that you are hearing the voice of God. Do not pass judgements on your sisters but love them unconditionally as I have loved you.

Love, Sophia

Each sister slept a little lighter and more peacefully that night with the promise of new adventures and change in the air.

The next day the sisters woke up, enjoyed a breakfast of fruit, bacon, eggs, and grits. Afterward they headed to the beach. The sunny day had a mild breeze, and the cool, crisp sand felt good beneath their feet. It was the perfect beach day. They set up their tent, umbrellas, and chairs and got ready for relaxing. Victoria wanted to walk, and Carmen decided to join her.

Victoria

Victoria still looked sickly from the emotional toll of her marriage falling apart, but her face showed signs of becoming fuller, and her outlook was improving. These last several days she was eating more, stressing less, and sleeping better. Carmen could see the improvement this trip was already having on her sister. Being heavily involved with church had helped her with maintaining her active lifestyle. She was at least glad for that. However, that maintenance had come with a great deal of sacrifice: the sacrifice of her marriage. She and Grant were on two different spectrums, the proverbial ships passing in the night. Really, ships, she thought. Just as wide and as vast as the ocean Carmen and her were currently passing, so was how far she felt from Grant. How did it get like this? She became tearful.

Carmen noticed and asked, "Sis, what's up?"

Victoria paused. "I just don't understand how it got like this. I mean I do all the right things—go to church, attend Bible study, and love the Lord dearly—but my husband couldn't even bear to see me off. It's not just me I'm concerned about; it's our daughter as well. He doesn't even care about her well-being. This has been the hardest pregnancy. It's really taken a toll on me emotionally," she lamented.

Carmen was pensive. She didn't know what to say to her sister. What could she say? She had a mess of her own. So, she just listened until Victoria got quiet. They walked up the beach, each contemplating their own situation.

Linda

Back at "camp" where the sisters had everything set up, Sophia and Linda spent the morning and part of the afternoon catching up on each other's kids and careers. Then, the conversation turned to marriages.

"I can't believe our ten-year anniversary is coming up," Sophia reminisced.

"Me either," Linda offered. "It was just yesterday you two met."

"I know. Thank you for introducing us." Sophia was forever grateful that Linda had introduced her and Sam. "I think we are going to renew our vows. I've been thinking a lot about it, and it seems like the way to go."

Linda smiled and started thinking out loud. "I wish Trent and I were planning to renew our vows. Instead, we might be getting a divorce."

Sophia was at a loss for words momentarily. "Linda, what in the world is going on?"

"A lot and nothing much at the same time," she responded. "We barely speak to one another unless it's about the kids. We barely see each other, and we are definitely not as close as we used to be. We stopped hanging out with other couples who had healthy marriages and made their marriage a priority over hanging out at business meetings and dinner affairs. It's a wonder we lasted this long." Her words hung in the air like thick clouds.

She began to jot her thoughts in her journal.

> *Today we are at the beach. I used to go to the beach with Trent all the time. We could sit and look at the ocean for hours without saying a word. Then, when we had kids, we would take them almost every Saturday to pick up shells, sort of a family tradition.*
>
> *That's about the time I met Dena. Wow, Dena and Fred had everything—the nice house, the best schools for their kids, cars, jewelry, vacations, and Dena stayed home. I decided that was the life I wanted to live, so to get there I would work extra hard a few years and then stay home. Only trouble is, I became addicted to success, money, and status. The business dinners, mergers, acquisitions, bonus checks. I love it all, and now I realize that this love slowly took the place of my family, especially my marriage. Trent and I have been married seven years and have taken only one vacation by ourselves: our honeymoon. How sad. What a sad way to live. How do I get out of this cycle?*

Sophia

Well, God, it seems everyone is getting along and really taking this trip seriously. I hope when the therapist comes she can also help us to see deeper and dig deeper into you. I appreciate you giving me this opportunity to invest in my sisters. I love them so much. What do you have for me God? It feels I have become so stagnant in my walk with you and my marriage.

At that moment she felt a stirring in her soul. One she had felt only when she had been pregnant. Sophia quickly dismissed the notion for several reasons but most of all because she and Sam were not "trying." In fact, they did the opposite of try; they followed God's lead. They always found it amusing when people asked them how many kids they wanted, when and if the next one was coming. They knew all too well it was really not in their hands but His, right where it belonged. She smiled at the possibility.

The next day was a relaxing, uneventful day. Each sister spent time reflecting and doing her own thing. Linda and Carmen went to town for some supplies just after lunch for everybody while Victoria stayed back at the beach house relaxing. Sophia was busy on the phone making the final arrangements with the Christian counselor. After that, she took a nice long nap the rest of the afternoon.

Victoria

God, I really enjoyed the beach with my sisters yesterday. It was so good to walk. I appreciate everything you've done for me. I love you so much. I feel our baby growing inside of me each and every day. I wish Grant was here, and we were on the same page. We used to be a "power couple." I love that man, but he drives me crazy! That's probably why I love him. One minute he is gung ho to do mission work and then the next he wants to slow things down because our daughter is on the way. I fell in love with him because of his ability to be flexible in his thinking and commitments but now I'm wishing he was more committed to one course of direction for longer periods of time instead of changing plans and his mind almost weekly. I can't believe we are expanding our family together, but this is not how either of us planned it. We were supposed to be a team, us against the world, not us against each other. God, I need you to work a miracle in our hearts right now. Without it we will cease. I need my husband back in my life. Show me what to do, Lord, show me!

Victoria was desperate and began to sob. This had been building up a long time. She needed the release. The grief was overwhelming, but from her life experience of watching her sister Sophia deal with grief she knew that to move forward she must let go, let go of her preconceived notions of how things were supposed to be. She had always thought ministering together would be a blessing to her family and she did not want to give it up. But she may have to. She really needed to dig into God's Word and see what plans he has for her family. She also needed to forgive Grant for abandoning her...something she was not ready for.

Linda

After returning from her shopping excursion with Carmen, all Linda wanted was a nap. She had noticed during this trip just how tired she was. She took a few moments to write in her journal first.

Well, it's good being here and gaining some perspective on my current situation. I never realized how tired I have become. I mean this is crazy. I guess while I've been going a million miles an hour it never really hit me. It must be exhausting for Trent to see me like this. I wonder what the kids are thinking. This is crazy! I can't continue to live my life like this. I'm getting old, and I don't want to! When am I going to enjoy everything I worked for? She wrote angrily. *And who's going to share it with me when it's time to enjoy it? Trent is ready to leave—the man who doesn't even joke about divorce and gets pretty upset when anybody does. Then there are the kids. They will leave soon. Am I to be all alone with my mergers and acquisitions?* It was a question Linda needed to ponder.

Carmen

Carmen had really been trying to distract herself. In fact, every time she had a free moment, she would just stare at her journal. The blank pages haunted her. She had enough words to fill a novel but was not ready to record the unthinkable tragedy that was her life currently. I mean, really, who comes back from her honeymoon to find out her husband not only cheated on her but lied about his kids? How could you do that? A direct violation of trust. At this point her vows meant nothing. Absolutely nothing. She stared at her journal for a good long time, and she wept. Today's journal entry held all her tears and pain. She cried herself to sleep.

Sisters

The next afternoon the house was abuzz with the anticipation of meeting the Christian marriage counselor. Each woman was anxious with anticipation about what the session would bring and how it would go. They met in the living room with their journals, water, and tissues. All of them had been crying at one point or another. Carmen's eyes were still red and swollen from weeping and crying out to the Lord yesterday.

Martha Turner arrived at two sharp. The tall, slender middle-aged woman smiled when Sophia answered the door and came right in ready to work. Her almond eyes shone as she explained a little about herself, how she had been a marriage and family counselor for over twenty years in a practice that was continuing to grow as well as telling them she had been married over fifteen years and had three children. Then, she explained, "Ladies, we will have two sessions. This first session will help us get to know each other as well as areas we need to work on in your marriages. We will talk, do an activity, and then I will end with one-on-one time with you in which I will customize your homework. Let's get to work."

She passed out a blank piece of paper to each sister. "I would like each of you to take a few minutes to draw one item that represents you and then think about why it represents you, and then we will share with the group."

At first each sister hesitated, thinking, I thought we were supposed to be working on our marriage. Martha Turner had seen these looks before. She immediately chimed in, "A good marriage is made of two whole people, not just half individuals looking for the other to fulfill their needs." Wow, Carmen thought and jotted this down in her journal before she started to draw.

After about ten minutes, the women were done. Carmen went first. "I drew a unicorn because it's whimsical, and that's how I wish my life was now. Carefree and easy. My life is anything but carefree and easy."

Sophia went next. "I drew a beach house. I love the calmness of the beach and how you have to cross the prickly sand sometimes to get to the peacefulness of the ocean. The house represents a place of refuge for me when it's all said and done. Its home; it's my family—my husband, kids, and me.

Linda shared hers. "I drew a pogo stick! Right now my life is so up and down, and I'm struggling trying to balance it all. I want help. I want balance. I'm sick of this."

Victoria spoke next. "I drew an eraser. This eraser would allow me to do over some things, situations, and actions in my marriage and life. I would love to erase it all and start over." She trailed off.

Martha asked each sister to write down her insights into her journal so they could go back and do a further review of them later.

Next, she had the sisters split up in pairs. Carmen and Sophia were paired together, making Victoria and Linda partners for the next activity. She wanted each sister to take ten minutes and point out to the other sister some pitfalls and solutions to the problems she was having. The sister not talking was to listen and just jot down notes in her journal.

Sophia began to speak to Carmen, but before she could get started, Martha gave further insight into the pairing. "I placed you two together because I think you can balance each other well. Sophia, you need more adventure and spontaneity in your life. You have always been consistent, but that seems to bore you right now. Carmen is energetic, as evidenced by her unicorn drawing, but with that she needs to calm down and stop running long enough so she can be insightful and do what's best. Sophia, that's what you do best and your drawing of the beach house represents that attribute well."

"How insightful," the sisters said in unison out loud. Who knew so much had already been accomplished in half an hour? Martha moved on to Victoria and Linda.

"The reason I put you two together is because you have similar situations. You both have run from your problems in your marriages instead of dealing with them head on. Linda, you drown yourself in work at the cost of your family, and that's why you feel like you're on a pogo stick you can't get off of. Victoria, same with you and the eraser. You want a do over, yet you keep doing the same thing, running to do church activities and work instead of ministering to your own family. When is the last time you talked to God before making a move?"

"I will set the timer," Martha said. "Remember, you have only ten minutes to speak and for the other to listen. Choose your words carefully and begin."

Sophia

"Carmen, I see you struggling. You're newly married, and then this happens, but you are not as powerless as you think. A lot can be said for getting on your knees and praying like Mommy and Daddy taught us growing up. Sometimes you don't know what to say, so you just say amen. God knows everything you think before you even think it. He created you. Seek Him, daily. He will speak truth to you more intimately than any person on earth can.

"I love you, sister, and am here for you, but you made a vow for better or worse. Sickness or health. Richer or poorer. And I'd say right now your marriage is on life support. You are experiencing the 'worse,' 'sickness,' and 'poorer,' but take heart. You have the Ultimate healer living on the inside of you."

Victoria

"Linda, I see you, and I'm jealous. You have a doting husband and great children, but yet you don't spend time with them? I wish I had that. You gave it all away for money, accolades, fame? I don't get it. Trent takes excellent care of your family, but it's like you spit in his face by not being content with what he is providing. You used to be happy. Now you are angry, and your lifestyle is catching up with you. It's taken a toll on your health, your marriage, and other relationships. It's time to make a choice once and for all that places your family first and your work secondly. I believe once you put your family first everything else will fall into place. You also need to think about what legacy do you want to leave?"

"Time," Martha interjected.

Carmen

"Sophia, I envy you. I mean you have it all together, but I know life's tragedies have left you jaded, sister. My hope for you is to be more carefree, spontaneous even. I know losing your child has made you more cautious and see the world for what it tragically is but that's not living that's just existing and there are still beautiful experiences to be enjoyed here on earth. Maybe one day Sam and you should just go to the beach without much notice or take the kids on a surprise getaway. I pray all is well and that you can truly enjoy every moment just like you learned to do right after Michael died."

Linda

"Victoria, to be young in your marriage again before all the damage of life and bitterness took root in your marriage that, my sister, is my hope for you. First babies bring so much joy, yet you all are in turmoil. Don't waste your marriage and opportunity by spending every waking moment at church. There must be balance, but more importantly, God, not other people, must guide your marriage.

"I encourage you to seek his counsel on what you should do each day before your feet hit the ground. He will direct your paths. I also encourage you to start praying and dreaming with Grant again, the way you all did when you were newlyweds. Never lose that. Never lose the essence of what makes you all you."

"Time," Martha announced.

Sisters

Each sister was emotionally spent, but they had made much progress. They enjoyed refreshments of tea and finger sandwiches Sophia had prepared earlier. And as they settled down after their snacking Martha met with each sister one on one to give her assignments for the week. Martha spent some one on one time getting to know more about each sister, their marriages, and the struggles they were facing before she gave their assignments for the week. To Carmen she said to write down all the reasons she loved Kelly and then write down all the reasons she felt betrayed by him on separate pieces of paper. After that she wanted her to spend some serious time alone without the influence of her sisters or others as to why she would go back or if she would go back. Prayer, Martha said, would be the key to her assignment.

She wanted Sophia to write sixty items she had always wanted to do but never had, or thought she never had, the time, energy, or resources to do. Thirty of those items needed to be done exclusively with Sam.

Linda's assignment was to paint a picture of how she saw her life in twenty years and who was in it. She was to go get some art supplies and let the creativity flow.

Victoria's assignment was to write the birth plan she had in mind and how she planned to incorporate Grant. Victoria was skeptical because her assignment seemed so simple. Martha assured her that on the surface it may appear that way, but deep down the assignment would reveal layers she had not thought of before.

Martha Turner left shortly after giving out their assignments and said she would be back next week. Each sister wanted and needed to rest. They each retired to their rooms and slept in peace for the rest of the afternoon until there was an unexpected knock at the door.

"I need to speak with her immediately!" A man shouted, "Somebody let me in!"

Sophia arrived at the door first with her sisters right behind her. They all gave each other perplexed looks. Who could be calling on them, only their family knew where they were. Sophia peeked out the window as the others stood behind her for back up. She saw a sight that was quite amusing: a grown man kneeling on the ground with hands clasped and pleading to be let in. It was Grant.

Victoria

After the commotion, the others went back to their rooms to get ready for dinner in town. Victoria stayed and talked to Grant.

"I'm so sorry, baby," he started. "I don't know what I was thinking. I love you. I love our daughter. I love our family. I became too prideful wanting things only my way. I now regret that. And to not be with you at the doctors...unforgivable."

Victoria was speechless. Was this the same man who had been giving her ultimatums? What or who had changed him? Right now she didn't care. It felt good to have her husband back. That night she enjoyed sleeping next to Grant after months of sleeping alone.

The next morning Grant left after breakfast. He reassured Victoria she should continue this journey she was on and that they would talk when she got back. *Reassured* and *Grant*, two words she thought she would never use in the same sentence. She got her journal.

God, I can't believe Grant was here. That he surprised me
like that. I'm not quite sure what to make of it. Could we
really be in love again, or was I dreaming, and why did
he keep talking about a Dawn he met at the new church
he is going to?

"Dawn suggested I reach out to you," she recalled Grant
saying last night. Dawn, this Dawn that is he sleeping with or
worse, she thought having an emotional affair? "Just like you
are with church," she heard God say. Ouch! That convicted her.

Sophia

What a whirlwind of events. First the therapy session,
then Victoria's husband popping up!

W hat's next, Lord? Are Kelly and Trent on their way?" she
asked jokingly. Well, I need to be more adventurous,
spontaneous even…less…predictable? She started making a
list in her journal of things she always wanted to do: horseback
riding, skydiving, whitewater rafting, rushing a football field,
run a half marathon, taekwondo, kickboxing… She started
another list, "places I want to travel to," and included Paris,
Greece, Africa for a safari, and Aruba.

Linda

Linda spent the next few days painting her picture. She started with a beach house. Not only did she love the beach and how tranquil it was but she planned to own one in the next twenty years. Then, she painted the yard with a garden and then herself and her two children. She stopped. Would Trent be in her life and if he was, in what capacity? Twenty years from now was a long time. She would come back to that.

Carmen

I hate Kelly!!!!!!!! I really hate him! God, how could he use me and mistreat me? Why? And what about his kids how do they fit into the equation? I love him. I think he is the most kindest, sweetest person I know. Or at least I thought he was. I need him... No, I need you. God, please help. What am I supposed to do????

Victoria

Birth Plan:

Husband present: possibly
Sisters present: definitely
Epidural: if I need it
Natural Labor: as long as possible
C-section: If baby's in danger
Incorporate husband by: ?

Sisters

It had been one week since Martha's first visit. The house was abuzz with each sister eagerly anticipating her arrival and the new insights she would bring as well as making last-minute touches to their assignments. This time Martha said she would meet first with each sister individually, and then they would all participate in a group activity. Victoria was first.

Victoria

"So, Victoria," Martha started, "how was your birthing plan?" Victoria immediately jumped in and told Martha how she felt about Grant's visit and how it made the situation harder when she saw how he actually cared for her. She also said she was upset about his mentioning another woman. As far as her birthing plan, Grant still had a limited, if not nonexistent, role. Martha suggested Victoria process her feelings about Grant, his visit, and Dawn before she revised her birth plan. She encouraged Victoria to take a few days before she made any final decisions. Victoria agreed.

Linda

Linda came in next. "So, Linda, how was painting your picture?"

"It was awesome, very therapeutic," she said enthusiastically. "I mean I don't remember the last time I had so much fun, and I've been sleeping better."

"That's awesome," Martha replied. "Let's see the portrait."

She studied the blue beach house with white shutters and a red roof with Linda, her two kids, and Trent outside it. Trent's arms were around Linda's waist, and she was glowing. The kids were older and appeared to be approaching or leaving, depending on how you viewed the picture. Linda explained that after much thought, it came down to her heart. She wanted her marriage and relationship to Trent more than anything.

"I'm very impressed with your progress and insight, Linda. I want you to keep painting more paintings of what your life looks like and how Trent and you can get back to loving each other." Linda agreed. She was ready to explore her artistic side.

Carmen

Carmen walked in just as confused as she had ever been. She loved Kelly but hated his guts for what he had done to her. Or, had she done it herself by ignoring some glaring signs all in the name of love? First, there was the fact that at the mention of them starting a family, he would squirm. Physically squirm, to the point of being uncomfortable. Then, whenever they would talk about their past relationships, he would change the subject, stating it was too painful to discuss and that the only thing he had learned was his need to move on.

Carmen shared all this with Martha, who attentively listened but was not impressed by the circumstances. She had many years of counseling experience and this circumstance was bad although not extraordinarily tragic as she had seen worst cases with marriages that did repair. After she was done, Martha asked Carmen what she intended to do about her relationship.

"I don't know," she lamented. "Do I have to make a decision?"

"Yes," Martha replied. "Until you do, you will remain in a constant state of turmoil in many areas of your life."

Sophia

"Well, Martha, I started my list, and I've got to say I'm excited!" I can't believe all the things I've been putting off. I can't wait to share them with Sam. Now, as far as being spontaneous, I'm still working on that, but I have a surprise planned for Sam when we get back from the trip."

"Great! I'm glad to hear you taking the assignment so well. This week I want you to do the first thing that comes to your mind when you wake up, no questions asked or debating, and ask one of your sisters to come along with you. Also, continue writing your adventure list."

Sisters

The sisters and Martha met in the kitchen where she had an activity set up. She called it "I wish my marriage were/ my marriage is."

The sisters sat in a circle around the table, facing each other. In the center of the table were cards with different words on them.

"Now, I want you to pick five cards that describe your marriage today, and then I want you to pick five cards that describe the way you want your marriage to improve. They must be different."

Each woman carefully selected her cards, taking time to make sure the others didn't see. After about ten minutes, Martha instructed the women to reveal their cards.

Victoria started it off. Her cards were "rocky," "tenuous," "unpredictable," "shaky," and "second."

"These describe my marriage to Grant now. As everyone has seen, it's very unpredictable. One minute we aren't talking, then the next he is showing up here to surprise me. It also feels second best to church, ministry, and other people's needs."

Next, Victoria showed how she would like her marriage to be. The cards she picked were "safe," "loving," "joy filed," "first," and "stable."

"I want our marriage to be a safe place I can come too when the world gets too tough. I also want the stability of knowing no matter what we will stand together. It is us against the world, not us versus us!" The sisters all nodded in agreement. They each understood what she meant all too well.

Sophia went next. "The words that describe my marriage now are hopeful, consistent, predictable, boring, and transitioning. I would like my marriage to be more adventurous, spontaneous, passionate, solid, and joyful. I love Sam, but it feels like at times we have fallen in a routine that becomes monotonous. But things were heating up before we left, so I'm hopeful we will be able to continue that," she said smiling.

Carmen chimed in, "Right now my marriage is desolate, distraught, discombobulated, destructive, and downright disastrous. I can't stand it. I thought my marriage would be joyful, loving, passionate, fairy tale even, and perfect." It was too much for Carmen to handle; she ran out of the room in tears.

Sophia went to comfort her but quickly returned. Carmen wanted to be alone. Martha suggested they finish the exercise and then she would go talk to Carmen after she had some time to process her thoughts and feelings. All the sisters understood but knew on a deeper level that this situation was affecting Carmen deeply because she had an unrealistic expectation of marriage. She had been too focused on the wedding.

Linda proceeded. "Although my situation is not as dire as Carmen's, the cards I choose to describe my marriage currently are brutal, stale, stagnant, roommate-ish, and cold. I want a marriage filled with love, warmth, caring, partnership, and passion."

Martha said her goodbyes to the sisters and encouraged them to spend this last week at the beach working on their assignments and really digging deep into how they wanted their futures to look. She also said Carmen would need extra support both for this week and once they got back, and the sisters needed to hold each other accountable. They all agreed and thanked her immensely for the time she had spent with them.

Carmen

Martha found Carmen down by the seashore crying and in deep thought. She did not want to talk; she was too angry.

After a time sitting next to her, Martha spoke. "Carmen, I used to be like you. I was so caught up in my wedding day, the guest list, the party, the food, the honeymoon. There is nothing wrong with that, but I forgot about the marriage, and after about a month I had it with my husband."

"Everything he did drove me crazy. I threatened to leave him several times. Even removed my ring. Now, I'm not saying my newlywed growing pains compare to what you are experiencing. They don't, you are dealing with infidelity, a secret relationship, children, and trust issues on top of an already fragile situation. Did you all have premarital counseling?"

"No, we were supposed to, but didn't make time. All my sisters and family encouraged us, but we thought we didn't need it. Now I realize we did. I wish I could start over."

"You can," Martha said assertively, "but you have to decide how you move forward. You have two choices: continue to live in this moment of turmoil or move on however that means for you. But you cannot do both. If you decide to move forward with your marriage, it will be hard. You will want to give up, but anything worth having is worth fighting for. If you leave, it will also be hard and hard for you to trust the next man who comes into your life. Part of you will always be wondering if he is trustworthy or if he is lying to you unless you truly move forward."

"Either choice requires you to not live in this moment. Living in this pain continuously will continue to wreak havoc on you. Love yourself enough to choose and not let circumstances choose for you."

"This week I want you to get in your Bible and pray like you never have before. Fast even. Dig into God's Word and see what He says about you individually and then you as a married couple."

"OK."

"I would like to see you for individual counseling when you get back, and I have a recommendation for you for marriage counseling once you've made your decision."

Martha Turner left, and Carmen was left with her thoughts. She sat on the beach until sunset and then returned to the beach house. She had a lot to think about, but the shore had made her calm, and for that she was thankful.

Sophia

The next day Sophia woke up, and first thing she wanted to do was read her Bible on the beach with the sunrise. She quickly dressed and invited Carmen. She opened her Bible to Jeremiah 29:11-14, and Carmen smiled. She knew this verse well. It was, after all, her life verse. It gave her peace when nothing else would. God knew the plans He had for her. She just needed to get on the same page as Him.

Carmen silently prayed to God right then. Dear God, you know your plans and thoughts toward me, but right now I am lost. I am married and considering a divorce. I love Kelly, but the pain is unbearable. My heart is broken. How can I ever love him, trust him, be intimate with him again? Have kids and a life with him? It's completely out of the question. Give me guidance and the courage to know what to do. Amen.

They watched the sunrise and headed "home" to the beach house to join the others for breakfast. Sophia felt refreshed and exhilarated and thankful her sister was there with her.

Victoria

Once all the sisters were back at the beach house, Victoria informed them she was starting to feel uncomfortable. She wanted to see if they could cut the trip short and spend only a few days at the resort. They all agreed. They all wanted to get back to their lives, families, and routines. Each had a desire to start to use the insights she had learned on this trip including Carmen.

Victoria decided after breakfast that she needed to know the nature of Grant and Dawn's relationship before she passed judgement or made any decisions, so she phoned home.

Grant answered on the first ring. "Hello." He sounded cold, distant.

"Grant, this is Victoria."

"I know."

"The reason I'm calling is while I enjoyed seeing you, I'm troubled by your frequent mention of Dawn."

"I'm sorry, Victoria. Things have gone too far. It started out very friendly, but then I became emotionally involved. I mean, she listened to me, had time for me, made me laugh even. This is not an excuse, but that's how things went wrong. I thought I could handle a platonic relationship with someone of the opposite sex that you didn't know, but I see I was wrong. I realized after I left just how much I was talking about her. That is not fair to you, my wife. She's here now. I'm telling her we can no longer be friends."

"You couldn't do that over the phone?"

"Yeah, I should have. I guess I thought it would be better in person."

"Have you two been physically intimate?"

"No, I swear to you that in that aspect I have been faithful, but I regret allowing another woman in my heart. For that I'm truly sorry."

She hung up the phone. She knew Grant well enough to know he was telling the truth. He may be a lot of things, but a liar was not one of them. She was ready to move forward.

Carmen

Carmen was ready to move forward as well. She missed Kelly, but the pain still had its sting. She did agree with Martha about one thing. She needed to be in counseling. She began to journal her feelings.

> *So I finally made a decision in this situation. I want to continue individual counseling and see where that takes me. I know it's taboo, but sometimes it's good to talk to someone with an objective perspective. Martha is excellent, insightful, and thorough. I'll be in good hands. I feel working on myself and my expectations will help me decide if I want to move forward with Kelly or not. I know he comes with a lot of baggage. Am I willing to be a stepmother? Willing to provide emotionally, spiritually, physically, and financially to children who are not mine? And what kinds of challenges will we be facing? I wanted to have kids of my own someday.*

One thing was for sure. Carmen had matured over the last several weeks.

Linda

Linda spent the next several days painting. Sometimes she painted how she felt about a sunset or the moon. Other times she painted Trent and her on motorcycles or flying an airplane together. In each picture they were so happy, smiling, beaming really, from ear to ear. So how could she get back to the loving in her marriage? One day at a time.

She noticed that if she went back, she could pinpoint where things had gone south. They had stopped kissing and flirting with each other. Yes, they had still pecked each other, but there was no passion. She decided that from here on out when she kissed Trent, she would kiss longer and intimately, flirting with him as well. The more they grossed their kids out, the better. Then she would know they were on the right track. She had grown up in a house where affection was not readily displayed, so it was a struggle for her to do so, but she was going to make the effort!

Sophia

S ophia was enjoying waking up and doing whatever she pleased. So far she had a sunrise Bible study, breakfast on the beach, gone for a midnight ocean swim, and slept in. With the exception of sleeping in, one of her sisters had joined her, and it was so exhilarating! She had to find a way to continue the fun with Sam once she got home. On the weekends they would definitely do bigger spontaneous adventures together or with the kids. During the week, little things like breakfast in bed could be done. She was so excited that she started adding more adventures to her list; such as going to *Christmas, FL and mailing her Christmas cards from there one year, scuba dive, get a dog, go camping in a national park, take a road trip across the country and up the coast, drive to the middle of nowhere just for some good food, and go to the home of BBQ which she believed to be Texas.*

The time wound down with each sister enjoying the last of her days at the beach house. The last night they had another jazz party in the living room. This time they felt lighter, happier, renewed. They were ready to face their new lives once they returned home.

The next morning, after loading the car, they drove the short thirty minutes to the resort. It was gorgeous. They decided to stay in a suite since they would be there only a few days. Sophia encouraged everybody to relax and enjoy the spa services. Victoria said she was ready but had one thing to do before she could get a massage. She said she would meet Sophia there later.

Victoria

Birth Plan:
Present: Grant and sisters

Incorporate husband by allowing him to have an active role such as coaching me with breathing and relaxation, also cutting baby's cord and placing her on me.

She smiled.

She arrived just as her sisters Sophia and Linda had started their massages. It was wonderful. She did not realize how much pressure and tension her body had been under these last months. She melted on the table.

Carmen

Carmen was not one for massages, but facials were her thing. She went to the facial spa where she enjoyed a hydrating mask and face moisture lift. She felt like a million bucks. Next, she caught up with her sisters to enjoy manicures and pedicures. They enjoyed jovial girl talk, and she started to feel like herself again.

Linda

Linda could not remember the last time she was this relaxed. She was really enjoying it. Her breakneck schedule had not allowed her to do this in a while. She needed more of this, but the only way she saw that happening was to cut back working. She would be free for her family. Several weeks ago she would never have considered this, but now she knew it was both possible and necessary. Her family and Trent needed her, not the money.

Sophia

Sophia beamed from ear to ear. Thank you, God, for allowing me to facilitate this opportunity for my sisters. It's just what we needed. Look at their smiling faces, she thought.

Sisters

After spa days, massages, laughs, and girl time, they checked out on Monday morning. The journey back home seemed quicker than when they had first started out and was also highly anticipated. Each woman was met by her husband and family at Sophia's house except Carmen. She was still not ready to see Kelly until she worked on herself. The first thing she did when she got back was call Martha and set up her first individual appointment the following week. She then called Kelly and let him know she had made it back safely.

Sophia

Sophia leapt into Sam's arms when she returned home. This was the longest they had ever been apart, and she missed him tremendously. She wanted to tell him everything that had happened and how she thought their lives would change for the better. Sam smiled lovingly at her enthusiastic attitude.

Linda

The car ride home was less tense than the previous one had been. Linda was glad. Trent had actually missed her. He couldn't resist hugging her when he saw her. The kids' spirits were lifted. They loved seeing their parents happy together even if it grossed them out.

Once home, Linda showed Trent the paintings and her journal. She explained what it meant. The main point was that she loved him and couldn't live without him.

Trent smiled. "This is what I wanted all along, for you to fight for our marriage. I'm glad you are home."

Linda hated to ruin the mood, but she needed to know about the divorce papers.

"We can talk about that. I never wanted to divorce you, but it was the only way I thought I could get your attention."

"Next time, let's agree on other ways to get each other's attention before divorce is mentioned."

"Ok," Trent agreed.

They also both agreed to seek a marriage counselor to maintain their relationship and make sure it was right on track.

Victoria

Grant had called Victoria before she left the resort, and they agreed he could pick her up. When they saw each other, it was like seeing the love of their lives for the first time. It was powerful, and neither one of them had experienced it before.

As they drove home together, which Victoria never thought would happen, they talked and caught up. They agreed a lot had transpired and needed to be changed. First and foremost, they needed to be together and work together. Others were not to become before their marriage. After their relationships with God, they were each other's next priority. Victoria agreed to step down at church from most of the activities she was involved in. She would pick one or two of them to give her attention to. Grant would do the same, and they wanted to try to find something inside or out of church they could do together to connect. They enjoyed the rest of the ride home.

Sophia

Six months had passed since the sisters went on their retreat. They had spoken often and done mini get-togethers as much as possible since they returned. One of their get-togethers was the birth of Victoria and Grant's daughter, Bella Rose. She came early one morning a week or so after the sisters had returned home. The doctor had threatened Victoria with a C-section, but with Grant there she was able to stand her ground and got an ultrasound to confirm the cords location; it was no longer around her neck, as well as a few moments to see if she could push Bella out. They prayed, and miraculously Bella was born happy, healthy, and without incident. This story always made Sophia smile.

Sophia was smiling a lot these days. She and Sam had been on several adventures, but her favorite one was their trip to Paris three months ago. That was when she learned they were expecting another miracle. Although Sophia had her doubts sometimes, her faith carried her through. Sam came up behind her as she looked in the mirror. He wrapped his arms around her growing belly. He softly whispered, "Time to get ready for the party." She smiled. All her sisters and their families were coming over for a BBQ.

Victoria, Grant, and Bella were the first to arrive. She couldn't believe her niece was six months already. Time was flying. Victoria had joined the new moms' group at church, Mom Connection while Grant headed the new dads' group. They were thriving and enjoying each other's company. Bella sure was beautiful.

True to form as the eldest sister, Linda arrived with enough food to feed an army, but she was happy. She smiled from ear to ear and glowed. I guess a trip to Hawaii and a restored marriage would do that to a person, Sophia thought.

Trent was jovial and enjoying spending time as a family. Linda had stepped down from her hectic work schedule and did not do business deals on the weekend. It wasn't always easy, but she found when she honored her vows, it always worked out. The kids loved having their family back together and their mom's home-cooked meals. Lasagna was still their favorite.

Sophia's baby sister, Carmen, was last to arrive. Sophia wasn't sure she was even going to make it with everything she had going on. Carmen had been busy doing individual and marriage counseling. She had learned a lot about herself and was maturing each and every session. Sophia beamed when she opened the door and saw Carmen and Kelly standing there. She saw love from them both.

"Who do we have here?" Sophia smiled.

"I would like to introduce you to Kelly's sons, Trey and William," Carmen said.

"This is our first family outing," Kelly added.

"Well, come on in, we have lots of kids you will enjoy playing with," Sophia responded.

It was beautiful, she thought. The four sisters each living out different marriages but with the same end goal in mind: to be pleasing in their Heavenly Father's eyes. Sophia chuckled. Marriage may be good, bad, ugly, and even downright crazy sometimes, but it was worth it.

CPSIA information can be obtained
at www.ICGtesting.com
Printed in the USA
LVOW12s2353300616

494819LV00014B/78/P